Based on the
ABC-TV Special
produced by D.I.C. Enterprises

Adapted by LORENTZ CARLSON

SCHOLASTIC INC.
New York   Toronto   London   Auckland   Sydney   Tokyo

ISBN 0-590-33149-3

12 11 10 9 8 7 6 5 4 3 2 1   3   4 5 6 7 8/8
Printed in the U.S.A.   18

Mrs. Evans came into the room. She was carrying a tray with a glass of milk and an apple. "Here, Henry," she said. "This will perk you up. You know what they say: 'An apple a day will keep the gloomies away.'"

Henry tried to smile, but he didn't feel like smiling. Suddenly a tear rolled from his eye and down his cheek. He ducked his head to hide it from Mrs. Evans. "I . . . I'm not hungry," he said.

The housekeeper placed the tray on an end table. She was upset because Henry was upset, but she didn't want him to know it. "I'm sure they'll find your mother and father soon, Henry," she said. "We'll all be back together again."

HENRY BIGG stood in his bedroom looking around. He couldn't believe what was happening. All of his posters, pictures, and pennants were down from the walls. There were half-filled suitcases on the floor. A large trunk, already filled and closed, stood near the door.

"Are you finished with your packing, Henry?" It was Mrs. Evans, the Bigg family's housekeeper, calling from the hall.

"Almost, Mrs. Evans," said Henry. He took some socks from his dresser and dropped them in the open suitcase.

Henry tried hard not to cry in front of Mrs. Evans. "I . . . hope so," he said.

Mrs. Evans picked up one of the suitcases. "I guess we'd better start putting your things in the car. Your Uncle Augustus is expecting you in an hour."

For a moment after Henry and Mrs. Evans left, the room was still and quiet. Then, suddenly, a panel in the ceiling began to slide open. When it was fully open, there was a hole in the ceiling just above the tray with the apple. A fork slid out of the hole. It was pointed toward the apple.

A voice came from inside the hole. "All clear! . . . Ready to launch the missile?"

"Ready!" came the answer.

"Fire missile!"

Zzzziipppp! The fork flew through the air and struck the apple, sticking in it.

"Bull's-eye!"

A string attached to the fork went taut. The apple was pulled off the

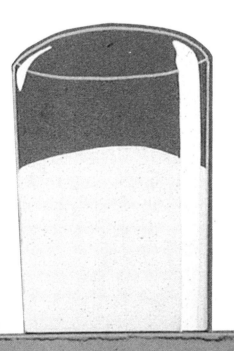

tray and into the air. It swung gently to and fro as it was pulled slowly up toward the ceiling.

Inside the ceiling were three tiny people pulling on the string which ran through a pulley. They were ten-year-old Tom Little, eight-year-old Lucy Little, and their grandfather, Adam Little.

The three Littles were part of a family of tiny people. The tallest Little was Mr. William T. Little, Tom and Lucy's father. He was only six inches tall. The tiny Littles lived in a small ten-room apartment inside the walls of a house owned by Henry's father. Mr. and Mrs. Bigg and Henry were regular-sized people. They didn't know the Littles were living in the house with them. The Littles were careful not to show themselves when the Biggs were around.

Even though they were small, the Littles looked quite a bit like ordinary people. The one big difference was — the Littles had tails!

At last, after much pulling and tugging on the string, the apple was out of Henry's room. It hung just below the pulley inside the ceiling.

"Hold her steady!" commanded Grandpa. Tom and Lucy braced themselves and held hard to the string. Grandpa let go. He pushed a wheelbarrow under the apple. "Okay," he said. "Now lower it into the wheelbarrow."

Tom said, "Wait 'til Mom and Dad see this apple. It'll last us for a month."

As the apple came to rest on the wheelbarrow, the two children jumped up on it and pulled out the fork.

"Poor Henry!" said Tom. "No wonder he doesn't feel like eating . . . having to live with an uncle he's never seen."

"How come?" said Lucy.

"Don't you remember?" Tom said. "His mother and dad got lost on an exploring trip."

"Sure I remember," said Lucy. "That's not what I mean. How come he's never seen his uncle when he doesn't live very far from here?"

"Augustus is a *creep*, that's why!" said Grandpa. "Mr. Bigg never liked him, even if he was his brother. They've had nothing to do with each other. It's a mystery to me why Bigg would let Augustus take care of Henry."

"I feel sorry for Henry," said Lucy.

"There's nothing we can do about it," said Grandpa. "We Littles can't get too involved. The big people might find out we're here."

When the apple was finally in the Littles' kitchen, it took up a good part of the room.

"Oh, Grandpa!" said Mrs. Little. "This is lovely! I hope you found a way to pay Henry back."

"We didn't," said Lucy.

"That's wrong," said Mr. Little. "It's one of our most important rules: We don't take things without trying to do a favor in return."

"But there isn't time to do Henry a favor," Tom said. "He's leaving today."

"Oh dear," said Mrs. Little. "I don't even like to think about it. What are we going to do with all the Biggs gone? How can we live here without them?"

"The first thing to do is to stay calm," said Mr. Little. "In my opinion, Henry's parents will be found and everything will turn out all right in the end. In the meantime we have enough supplies to last us for a while."

Suddenly the Littles heard Henry and Mrs. Evans talking as

they returned to the bedroom. Grandpa, Tom, and Lucy ran to the heating grate to listen.

"Why can't you come with me, Mrs. Evans?" Henry was asking.

"Your uncle made it perfectly clear he doesn't need a housekeeper," said Mrs. Evans. "But I'm sure he'll take good care of you. After all, he's your father's brother. And he's your guardian now."

"Only until they find my mother and father," said Henry.

Grandpa whispered angrily. "I know that Augustus like a book!" he said. "I lived in the walls of his house long ago. Believe me, no tiny person would live there for long. It's filled with rats and bats and giant beetles. He doesn't take care of the place. There are all kinds of creepy-crawly things."

"That's *awful!*" said Lucy.

"And so is that Augustus," Grandpa said. "He's as mean as they come."

In the meantime Henry was searching under his dresser. "Where can it be?" he said. "Where's my lucky rabbit's foot? I need it to bring Mom and Dad luck so someone will find them in that jungle."

"Maybe it's in the living room," said Mrs. Evans. "Come along — I'll help you look for it."

They started for the door.

"I saw his rabbit's foot last night," said Lucy. "It's under his bed."

"I've got a great idea how we can do Henry a favor," Tom said. "Let's put the rabbit's foot in his suitcase."

"Be very careful, children," said Mrs. Little, who was setting the table and listening. "You might be seen."

"Don't worry," said Grandpa. "I'll be watching them."

Grandpa and the children went up to the ceiling. As Grandpa watched from the open panel over

Grandpa whispered loudly from the ceiling, "Hurry! They could be back soon."

Tom climbed up onto the handle of the open suitcase. He was just below the rim. "Shove the rabbit's foot up here," he said to Lucy. "I'll drop it in the suitcase."

Lucy struggled to push the heavy good-luck charm up to her brother. When Tom got a firm grip on it, he pulled. It moved very little.

"Shove harder, Lucy," said Tom.

"You *pull* harder!" said Lucy, grunting. "I'm doing the best I can."

Henry's room, Tom and Lucy lowered themselves to the floor in a sugar bowl with a string attached to it.

Lucy led the way. They ran under Henry's bed and found the rabbit's foot behind a bed leg.

"Now," said Tom, "we have to hurry and get this into the suitcase before Henry gets back."

The children carried the rabbit's foot over to the chair where the open suitcase lay. With some effort they managed to climb the chair leg, dragging the rabbit's foot with them.

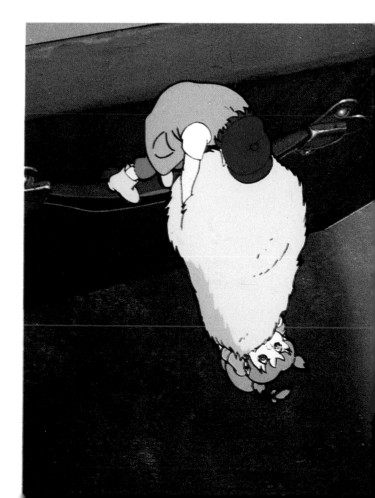

Finally Tom gave it his best try — a good, hard yank — and he pulled it up.

"That was tough!" Lucy said.

"Lucy, don't complain so much. It's not heavy. Watch!" The tiny boy lifted the rabbit's foot over his head. But he teetered back and forth with the weight of it.

"Tom, you'll fall!" said Lucy.

Tom laughed. "I never fall," he said. "I've got perfect . . ." The heavy weight of the rabbit's foot began to pull him over backward. ". . . balance!" he yelled, just as he teetered wildly and flipped over backward into the open suitcase.

Lucy scrambled up the handle and leaned over to help.

Suddenly they heard Mrs. Evans' voice. She was returning to the room with Henry. "I'll find your lucky rabbit's foot and mail it to you," she said.

Tom grabbed Lucy's hands. He was in too much of a hurry and, instead of pulling himself out, he pulled Lucy in!

"Kids!" whispered Grandpa from above. *Get out of there!*

The two big people entered the room. Tom and Lucy ducked in among the clothes.

Mrs. Evans closed the suitcase and the Littles were trapped.

IT WAS dark. The countryside was gloomy. Mrs. Evans and Henry drove in the car up to a large, dingy house. There was just one dim light in a top-story window. Near the house stood black trees with jagged branches.

"I'm scared, Mrs. Evans," said Henry. "It looks so gloomy."

Just as the car pulled up to the front door, a tough-looking, scroungy cat ran from the driveway and jumped up on a trash can. The lid clattered.

The dark shape of a figure appeared for a moment in the lighted window, then it was gone.

Mrs. Evans and Henry walked up the front steps of the house. Mrs. Evans banged the door knocker three times. Very soon, heavy, limping footsteps were heard just inside the house.

Henry took a deep breath.

The door creaked open. From out of the shadows there slowly came a man's dark, hunched figure, walking with a cane. When the moonlight struck the man's face, Henry gasped. It was the most unfriendly-looking person Henry had ever seen in his life. Could this be his uncle? He edged behind Mrs. Evans.

"H-how do you d-do," stammered Mrs. Evans. "I'm Mrs. Evans and this is Henry."

"Welcome, Henry," said the man. "I'm your Uncle Augustus." He held out his hand and smiled, but it wasn't a friendly smile.

Henry jumped back when he saw Augustus's bony hand coming toward him.

Mrs. Evans gently pushed Henry forward. "Shake hands with your uncle, Henry," she said.

"Hello, sir," said Henry, offering his hand.

They went to the car to pick up Henry's things. Tom and Lucy listened from inside the suitcase.

"I'm sure you'll be happy here, Henry," Augustus said. "Come along now." He patted Henry's head.

Once he got Henry inside the house, Augustus turned to shut the door. Henry and Mrs. Evans looked at each other across the doorway, tears in their eyes.

Augustus said, "Good-bye, Mrs. Evans," in his over-friendly voice. Then he slammed the door and bolted it.

Suddenly Augustus turned toward Henry and snarled, "Stop that sniffling! And get busy carrying your stuff upstairs."

"Y-yes, sir," said Henry. He picked up the suitcases as best he could. Augustus got hold of the large trunk and dragged it up the stairs, banging it from step to step. Henry followed slowly. He was struggling to hold all of the suitcases at the same time.

"Stop dawdling!" yelled Augustus. "Life isn't going to be soft for you anymore. My brother spoiled

you! But I'm your guardian now. We'll change all that."

From inside the suitcase, Tom and Lucy heard everything.

"Poor Henry!" whispered Lucy. "Stuck here with that awful man."

"We'll be stuck here too," Tom whispered, "if we don't find a way to get home."

Henry's room was dark, dirty, and dismal. There was dust all over the floor; cobwebs on the one wooden chair; bars on the windows.

Henry lugged the suitcases into the room. His uncle stood in the doorway. "Now put your clothes away," he said, then he stomped off.

"Yes, sir," said Henry. The boy was terribly sad and frightened. He wiped the tears from his eyes. Then he began to unlock one of the suitcases.

Inside, Tom and Lucy heard the clicking of the locks. They ducked down among the clothes as Henry opened the suitcase.

Henry saw his rabbit's foot right away. "Oh, good!" he said. "My lucky rabbit's foot! *Now* things will get better."

Just then Augustus called from the hall. "Henry! Come here."

Henry stuffed his rabbit's foot in his pocket and hurried from the room.

A few moments later two of Henry's socks seemed to jump out of the suitcase onto the floor all by themselves.

It was Tom and Lucy!

They stuck their heads out of the socks and looked around. Tom saw a crack in the baseboard. "We'll hop into that crack," he said. "Stay in your disguise, Lucy."

The tiny children began hopping across the floor in Henry's socks.

Just then, Augustus came walking into the room. He nearly stepped on the socks. Luckily he didn't look down. Tom and Lucy reached the baseboard and climbed out of the socks. They squeezed

the wall. They looked through the hole and saw Augustus and Henry sitting at a long table. There were bowls of soup in front of them.

"Eat your soup!" Augustus was saying to Henry.

"Excuse me, Uncle Augustus — but I don't like it very much," said Henry.

"Eat it!" roared Augustus. He slammed his fist down on the table. "*Force* yourself to eat it, like I'm forcing myself to put up with you!"

Henry put his spoon in the soup. "If you don't like me, why did you want to take care of me? I can live with Mrs. Evans. She likes me."

"*Liking* you has nothing to do with it," said Augustus. "I simply wanted to be appointed your guardian so I could be put in charge of your father's money."

through the crack and were safe inside the walls.

The two children began searching for Grandpa's old apartment. The place was scary. There was dust, cobwebs, and rusty nails in the passageways.

After an hour of looking, the children were tired and hungry and they had not found the apartment. Then they heard a strange slurping noise.

"What's that?" said Lucy.

"It's coming from over this way," said Tom. They followed the noise until they came to a small hole in

Henry was afraid of Augustus, but when he heard that he got angry. "My dad will get even with you when he gets back home."

Augustus smiled wickedly. He jumped up, knocking his chair over. "He won't have a home to get back to!" he yelled. Then he raised his cane over his head. "Two days from now I'm having bulldozers tear your house down!" He smashed the heavy cane down on the table, knocking his bowl and silverware to the floor.

"Tear down our *house*!" said Henry. "You can't do that! Why do you want to do an awful thing like that?"

"I'm going to put up a shopping center on the land, that's why!" Augustus said. "It's a perfect place for one. I'll make a bundle of

money!" Then he laughed. He pointed to the broken bowl and silverware scattered on the floor. "Now clean up that mess."

Inside the wall Lucy said, "Tom! He's going to tear down *our* house!"

"That guy's loony," said Tom. "We've got to get back home to warn Mom and Dad before those bulldozers crush them."

"But Tom, we're so far away."

"And we can't go at night," said Tom. "C'mon — let's find Grandpa's old place so we can get some sleep. We'll start early in the morning."

About ten minutes later the tiny children disturbed a sleeping rat. Rushing to get away, they tumbled down a hole and fell into a can.

"Hey! This is Grandpa's old tin-can elevator," said Tom.

In a moment they were going down through the walls. The elevator came to a stop at a tiny person's apartment.

"This is it!" Tom said.

"Where Grandpa used to live!" said Lucy.

They found some birthday candles and a box of matches. Soon they had the place lighted up so they could look around.

"It's awful dusty," said Tom, "but at least it's a place to spend the night. Tomorrow we'll head for home the fastest way we can find."

"But Tom, it'll take days to find our way," said Lucy.

"I know it," said Tom. "And by that time those bulldozers could be knocking the house down."

"With Mom and Dad and Grandpa inside," added Lucy.

They lay down in the bed.

"Hey, Tom," said Lucy after a moment.

"What?" answered Tom sleepily.

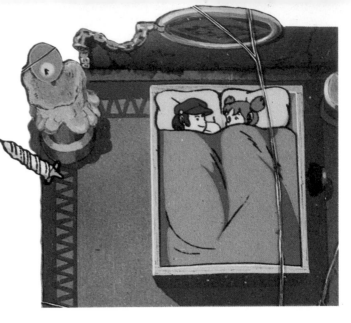

"Grandpa saw us get trapped, right?"

No answer.

"Then he knows where we are, right?"

Still no answer. Tom was asleep.

"He'll rescue us!" said Lucy firmly.

And with that thought, Lucy fell asleep too.

IT WAS early morning at the Biggs' house. A single shingle on the roof was lifted up. It was the Littles' secret shingle-door. Mr. and Mrs. Little and Grandpa climbed through to the roof.

Mr. Little looked at the sky. "He should be here soon," he said. "Cousin Dinky usually delivers our mail first thing in the morning."

"I do wish we could go too," said Mrs. Little. "I'm so worried about the children."

"It's best for Grandpa to go without us," said Mr. Little. "There won't be enough room in Dinky's glider for all of us to make the return trip."

"Besides," Grandpa said, "I'm the only one who knows the way. I lived there, remember?"

Mrs. Little pointed skyward.

"There he is!" she said.

It was Cousin Dinky's glider sailing through the air toward the roof.

The Littles waved. They were trying to signal Cousin Dinky to land (he usually dropped the mail in a net tied to the chimney).

When the glider pilot saw the Littles waving at him, he couldn't resist doing some stunts. He looped the loop and did a few tail-spins before he realized they wanted him to land.

The glider swooped down and landed on the roof. The Littles scattered as the glider bounced to a stop.

Before Cousin Dinky could get out of the cockpit, Grandpa jumped into the seat behind him. "Take off, Dinky!" he yelled. "We've got to rescue Tom and Lucy."

"W-what happened?" asked Cousin Dinky.

"I'll explain later — get this crate into the air," said Grandpa. "Move!"

"Roger!" said Cousin Dinky. He flipped his goggles back down over his eyes. "Pilot to navigator . . . check wind velocity . . . chart the course . . . keep me informed of the altitude."

"Navigator to pilot," said Grandpa. "Stop talking and take off!"

Mr. and Mrs. Little pushed the glider so that it was facing down the roof. It started rolling down the roof and sailed into the air.

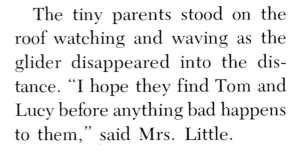

The tiny parents stood on the roof watching and waving as the glider disappeared into the distance. "I hope they find Tom and Lucy before anything bad happens to them," said Mrs. Little.

"It's Augustus!" said Lucy. "In two days he is going to send bull-dozers to knock down the Biggs' house — *our* house!"

"He wants to make a *shopping center* out of our house!" said Tom.

Grandpa shook his fist in the direction of downstairs. "You're a heartless old man, Augustus!" he said.

Just then Cousin Dinky climbed through the shingle-door into the attic. "Kids! What happened? What are you doing in this creepy house?"

"No time to talk, Dinky," said Grandpa. He headed for the shingle. "Let's go, kids! We've got to get that old crate back into the air."

"Hey! I just *got* here!" Cousin Dinky said.

Half an hour later Cousin Dinky and Grandpa were landing on the roof of Augustus's house. Tom and Lucy had found their way to the top floor, and were in the attic when Grandpa came climbing through his secret shingle-door.

They ran to him. "Grandpa! You found us!"

Grandpa gathered Tom and Lucy into his arms and gave them a big hug. "Are you okay, kids?" he asked.

"*We're* okay," said Tom. "But Mom and Dad are in big trouble unless we can get home in time to warn them."

Grandpa headed back out the shingle-door without answering. Tom and Lucy were right behind him. Cousin Dinky shrugged his shoulders and followed.

"Hold it!" said Grandpa. He jumped back from the shingle-door. "*Cat!*"

All three Littles peeked out and saw an alley cat on the roof. He was stalking the glider!

"No!" said Cousin Dinky. "That's not a bird!"

The cat jumped on the glider and broke it to pieces.

"There goes our ride," Tom said.

"How are we going to get home now?" asked Lucy.

"There's only one thing to do," said Tom. Before anyone could stop

him, he stepped out onto the roof and walked toward the cat. "I'm going to try to tame it. It will give us a ride home."

"Tom!" said Grandpa. "Get back here!"

"You heard your Grandpa!" shouted Lucy. She started after her brother.

"Stay back!" Tom said. "You'll scare the cat." Tom moved slowly toward the cat.

"Maybe he can do it," said Lucy. "Remember, he tamed the Biggs' cat."

"But this one's *an alley cat!*" said Grandpa. "They can't be tamed. At least I don't think they can."

Tom held his hand out. "Here kitty, kitty," he said. "Nice kitty."

The cat leaped toward the tiny boy.

"Tom!" yelled Lucy. "Oh, no!"

The cat was "playing" with Tom. He batted him back and forth between his paws.

"We've got to do something *now* to save Tom!" said Grandpa.

"Let's get out on the roof and play mouse," said Lucy. "Maybe the cat will forget about Tom when he sees us. When he comes after us, Tom can escape."

"It's worth a try," said Grandpa. He started out.

"Hold it!" said Cousin Dinky. "This is my game: adventure!" He jumped in front of Grandpa and ran onto the roof.

The cat stopped playing with Tom when he saw Cousin Dinky.

The tiny pilot sat on his haunches and squeaked like a mouse. The cat dropped Tom and ran after Cousin Dinky, who dived down the shingle-door.

"Maybe that did it," said Grandpa. But when he peeked out at the roof, the cat was still batting Tom around.

"Let's charge him all at the same time," said Grandpa, "and make a lot of noise. Yell, scream, bark like a dog."

The Littles climbed through the secret door. They lined up on the roof facing the cat.

"Go!" yelled Grandpa.

They ran toward the cat making all the fierce noises they could think of.

The cat picked up Tom in his mouth and ran up over the rooftop and disappeared.

FOR THE next ten minutes the Littles searched all over, looking for Tom and the cat. But they were nowhere to be seen.

"I can't believe it," said Cousin Dinky. "Tom's gone."

Lucy began to cry.

Grandpa put his arm around Lucy. They walked back to the shingle-door. "We did all we could," he said. "Being a tiny person is a hard life, Lucy, you know that. Now we have to get back home as soon as we can and save your parents."

They climbed through the door into the attic.

There was the cat, curled up on the floor. He had a contented look on his face. Tom's cap was lying nearby.

Lucy rushed over and picked up the cap. "You rat!" she said. "What did you do with my brother?"

Grandpa and Cousin Dinky tried to pull her away. "Lucy!" said Grandpa. "Stay back! Remember what happened to Tom."

Suddenly they heard Tom's voice coming from near the cat's stomach. "I'm over here." He sounded muffled.

"It swallowed Tom!" yelled Lucy. "He's talking. Tom — are you in there?"

No answer.

"Oh, Tom," said Lucy. "I'm *so* sorry! You were the best brother a girl ever had. Kind and good and brave. . . ."

Tom poked his head out of the cat's fur. "And smart too," he said. "I tamed the cat."

Lucy ran to her brother and hugged him.

"That wasn't funny, Tom," said Grandpa. "Lucy thought you were a goner."

"I was *sure* the cat swallowed you," said Lucy.

Tom held up a splinter. "Kitty wouldn't swallow me," he said. "I helped him by taking this splinter out of his paw."

"Tom!" said Cousin Dinky. "That is so corny! Who would ever believe that?"

Tom began laughing. "I know, I know," he said. "But it's *true*! Cross my heart."

"Good work, Tom," said Grandpa. "He'll get us safely back home."

"Right!" Tom said. Then to the cat, "Down, kitty!"

The cat crouched down. Tom, Lucy, and Grandpa climbed aboard. But when Cousin Dinky tried to get on, the cat turned and spit at him.

"Oh, oh!" said Tom. "For some reason he doesn't like you, Cousin Dinky."

Tom talked soothingly to the cat as Cousin Dinky sneaked onto the back of the animal.

"Okay," Grandpa said. "I think we can go now."

Tom — who was on the cat's neck — bent over and spoke into the animal's ear, "Okay, kitty — out the window."

The cat didn't move.

Tom pointed. "To the *window*, kitty," he said. *"Go out the window!"*

And still the cat didn't move.

"The window!" shouted Grandpa and Lucy.

The cat jumped, but in the wrong direction.

"This isn't going to work," said Grandpa. "We've got to figure out some way of getting him to go where we tell him."

"I've got an idea," said Tom. "I think it will work, but one of us will have to be awfully brave to make it work." He looked right at Cousin Dinky.

"Okay, Tom," said Cousin Dinky. "I'm fairly brave. What's your idea?"

A few moments later the cat was crouched on the attic floor. The Littles had put a blindfold over its eyes. Tom, Lucy, and Grandpa were tying the handle of a long paintbrush to the top of the cat's head.

The brush stuck out in front of the cat. Hanging from the brush was a swing made of pencil stubs — and sitting in the swing was Cousin Dinky!

"You're the *bait*," Tom explained to Cousin Dinky. "When we take off the blindfold, the cat will see you and try to go after you . . . I hope. That way we'll get him to move forward."

"I know, Tom," said Cousin Dinky. "I don't know how brave you have to be to do this. It seems to me it's more *foolish* than brave."

"It *has* to be you," Tom said. "You're the only one the cat doesn't like."

"Okay, kids — stop the gabbing," said Grandpa. "Let's test this out. As soon as you drop the blindfold, hop aboard quickly."

The blindfold fell. Seconds later Tom and Lucy were sitting behind Grandpa on the cat's back.

The cat saw Cousin Dinky and lurched forward toward him.

"He's moving!" said Grandpa. He was steering with the brush, wiggling it back and forth. Then he turned the brush toward the open attic window.

The cat rushed forward, trying to get at Cousin Dinky. He went out the window and up on the roof. He scooted across the shingles to a tree whose branches bent over the roof. Then, with a great leap, the cat made it to the tree. Grandpa

steered him right down to the ground.

"Make the cat head for home," said Cousin Dinky. "Let's get this over with."

"We're already heading that way," said Grandpa.

And, indeed, the cat with the Littles aboard was headed away from Augustus's house at a good speed.

Suddenly a mean-looking dog jumped from behind some bushes right in front of the cat.

The cat skidded to a halt. The two animals stared at each other.

"Oh, no!" Cousin Dinky said. "Caught between two beasts!" He closed his eyes.

The cat turned and ran back toward the house. The dog ran behind the cat, barking and growling and snapping at his tail.

"We're going the wrong way!" yelled Tom.

Grandpa twisted the brush handle back and forth. "I can't control him!" he shouted.

The cat darted back and forth between trees, trying to get away from the dog. It dashed through the gate into Augustus's yard. Suddenly, the cat saw an old wooden barrel lying on its side. The cat dived into the open end of the barrel. The Littles tumbled off. The dog jumped in right after the cat and the barrel broke into pieces.

The two animals kept right on running. Miraculously, none of the Littles was hurt.

THE LITTLES were still sitting, dazed, among the broken pieces of barrel when they heard Augustus's voice.

"Hurry it up! I haven't got all day!"

The tiny people looked and saw a moving van in front of the house. A man was pulling a trunk from out of the back of the van.

Henry rushed out of the house. "Oh, good! The trunk with my toys," he said.

"Toys!" roared Augustus. "Is *that* what this is? There's no time for toys around here. Get busy and mow the lawn."

Watching from the broken barrel, Tom remembered something. "Lucy," he said. "One of Henry's toys is that gas-powered airplane. We could get home on that."

Quickly, the Littles walked through the tall grass to the garage where the moving man was putting the trunk. They entered the garage as the moving man was leaving. The Littles soon discovered that the trunk was unlocked. It took all four of them to pull open the lid. The trunk was standing on end and some of the toys spilled out onto the garage floor. One of them was the toy airplane.

"Dinky, can you fly this kind of plane?" said Grandpa.

"I can fly anything with wings," said Cousin Dinky. He hopped into the cockpit.

Grandpa got in next to Cousin Dinky. Tom and Lucy sat behind them.

The plane's engine roared into life. The plane sped across the garage floor and into the air. It flew out the door upside down.

"How am I doing?" yelled Cousin Dinky.

"You're upside down!" Grandpa yelled back.

Cousin Dinky looked at the controls. "Wait a second," he said. "I must be doing something wrong."

The plane was headed for a tree. "Watch where you're going!" yelled Tom.

Lucy closed her eyes. "We're going to hit it!" she said.

The plane struck a limb of the

tree and spun out of control. Luckily, it fell into the tall, soft grass. The tiny people were thrown out, but no one was hurt.

While this was going on, Henry — who was cutting the lawn with the noisy lawn mower — didn't hear or see any of it. The plane crashed a few feet behind him. At the end of the lawn he turned and pushed the lawn mower back in the direction of the plane.

Tom and Lucy were the first to get to their feet after the crash. Tom saw the lawn mower heading toward them. "Let's get out of here!" he shouted. "We're going to be run over."

Lucy said, "We can't leave yet. Grandpa and Cousin Dinky are having some kind of trouble."

The two older Littles were struggling to get up. They were tangled in some weeds. Tom ran to help them.

Lucy could see there wouldn't be enough time unless she did something to stop Henry. She ran through the tall grass to where he was. As his huge leg came by she jumped on his ankle and bit him.

"*Ouch!*" said Henry. He stopped the mower. "Something bit me." Lucy jumped off and hid in the tall grass.

Tom looked up and saw Henry looming over him. He stopped trying to help Grandpa and Cousin Dinky, and ran to where Lucy was hiding.

Henry looked down and saw Grandpa and Cousin Dinky.

"Don't move, Dinky!" said Grandpa out of the corner of his mouth. The two tiny men froze.

As Henry stood looking, his uncle came up behind him. "What have you here?" he asked.

"I don't know, sir," Henry said.

Augustus squinted down at the motionless Littles. "Don't lie! You're playing with toys instead of mowing the lawn."

Henry said, "They're not mine." He looked again at the two tiny people. "Besides — they don't look like . . ."

Augustus interrupted Henry. "Give them to me!" He held out his hand.

Henry reached down into the tall grass and pulled Grandpa and Cousin Dinky out of the weeds.

He put them in Augustus's hand.

Lucy shut her eyes. "I don't want to look!"

Grandpa whispered to Cousin Dinky. "He thinks we're toys. Act like a toy."

The two Littles walked around Augustus's hand. They were stiff and straight — like windup toys.

"That's the last you'll see of these toys," said Augustus as he closed his bony hand around Grandpa and Cousin Dinky. Then he got hold of Henry's collar with the other hand. "And you'll spend the rest of the day in your room for lying!" He dragged Henry toward the house.

Tom grabbed Lucy's hand. "C'mon!" he said. They ran and jumped into Henry's pant cuff.

Augustus pushed, shoved, and dragged Henry into the house and up to his room. "Get in there, you little liar!" he yelled.

Henry stumbled toward the bed. "When my father gets back and finds out how you treated me, he'll . . . he'll . . . *beat you up!*"

"You're father is *never* coming back!" said Augustus.

"That's not true," said Henry. "And I don't believe he ever made you my guardian."

Augustus pulled a letter from his pocket. "I have proof," he said. "It's in your father's handwriting — look!" He shoved the paper at Henry's face.

Henry took one look and started to cry.

"And this letter gives me the right to do anything I want with your house too," said Augustus.

He stomped out of the room.

Henry flopped down on the bed sobbing.

Tom and Lucy climbed out of Henry's pant cuff and hid in a fold of the blanket.

"Poor Henry," Lucy whispered to Tom.

"And poor Grandpa and Cousin Dinky," whispered Tom. "How will we ever find them in this big house?"

"Maybe we'll have to get Henry to help us," said Lucy.

"Are you *crazy*?" said Tom, his voice getting louder. "Tiny people *never* talk to big people. For thousands of years they never have. Why should they now?"

"Because *I* don't know what else to do!" said Lucy crossly. "And we have to do *something*."

"Well, we're not going to do *that*!" Tom said.

"Tom!" shouted Lucy. She was staring straight ahead over Tom's shoulder.

"Quiet!" said Tom fiercely. "Do you want Henry to hear us?"

"T-Tom," said Lucy in a low voice. She pointed past her brother. "L-look!"

"Lucy — for crying out . . ." Tom turned his head to look where Lucy was pointing. ". . . loud!" he shouted.

The two tiny children were looking directly into the face of Henry Bigg, and he was looking directly at them.

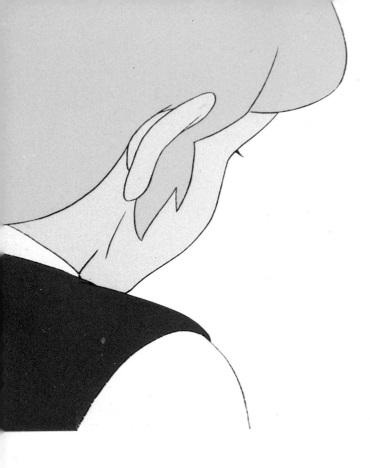

"HOLD still, Lucy," whispered Tom without moving his lips. "He'll think we're toys too."

Henry wiped his tear-filled eyes as if to see better. He bent over and looked closely at the two tiny children.

"Oh, Tom!" whispered Lucy. She was looking into Henry's eyes. "He *knows!*"

Then Henry said quietly. "You're real. You're like tiny, tiny kids. I heard you talking. You've got tails!"

Tom and Lucy stood stiffly, holding their breath, trying to look like toys.

"Toys can't talk like you can," Henry went on. "Talking toys don't sound real. *You* sound real."

"*Whoosh!!*" Tom and Lucy let their breath out together.

Tom put his hands on his hips and stuck his chest out. "Don't try anything, Henry," he said. "We're not helpless just because we're tiny."

Lucy slipped behind her brother. "Right!" she said. Then she whispered to Tom, "Don't get him angry."

"I *knew* you were real," said Henry, "but I couldn't believe it." He shook his head in amazement. "Oh, wow! Wait'll I tell my friends."

"Let's get one thing straight, Henry," said Tom, looking cross. "You're not going to tell *anyone* about us."

Henry smiled. "How could you stop me? You're so little."

"Little has nothing to do with it, Henry," said Tom.

"How do you know my name?" Henry asked. "Where do you come from? Why do you have tails?"

Lucy laughed. "Why don't *you* have a tail?" she said. "You look funny without one."

"Lucy, don't be impolite," said Tom.

"I still don't understand it," said Henry. "If you're real people, why are you so small?"

"We'll tell you all about us Littles if you help us find Grandpa and Cousin Dinky," said Tom. And he started telling Henry the whole story.

In the meantime, in another room of the house, Grandpa and Cousin Dinky were locked in a desk. Grandpa was trying to open the lock but with no luck. "It's no use," he said. "I can't budge it. There's got to be *some* way out. Dinky! Shine that flashlight over here."

Cousin Dinky was holding a small pocket flashlight he had found in the desk, and standing on some papers he was trying to read. "D—R—A—H—" he said to himself. He turned to Grandpa. "Forget that lock for a minute. Look at these letters written over and over again."

Grandpa walked to where Cousin Dinky was standing. "Will you please give me that flashlight?" he said. "I'm trying to get us out of here."

"I wonder why Augustus wrote this stuff," Cousin Dinky said.

"You're wasting our time, Dinky," said Grandpa. "We've got to get out of here."

Suddenly they heard a creaking door.

"He's coming!" said Grandpa. "It's make-believe-we're-toys time again."

The tiny people stood stiffly like two toys.

But it wasn't Augustus who came through the door. It was Henry, and he had Tom and Lucy with him! "This is the last room," Henry said. "If they're not here, they're not in the house."

Just then the phone on top of the desk began ringing.

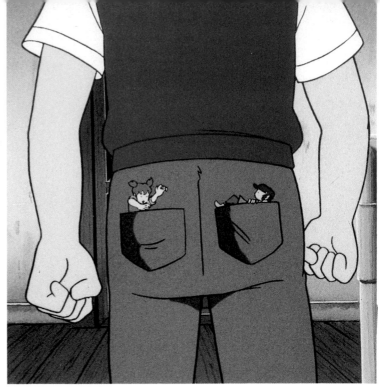

"Quick, Henry — hide!" said Tom. "The old grouch will be here to answer it."

Henry ducked behind a chair.

Augustus entered the room and switched on the light. He picked up the phone. "Yes?" he said. "You say your men will tear down the Biggs' house tomorrow? Good! How much is it going to cost me?

Wait! I'll get a pencil and write it down." Augustus turned to the desk and opened it with a key.

Lucy was the first to see Grandpa and Cousin Dinky standing like toys inside the desk. "There they are," she whispered.

Augustus sat at the desk. He took a piece of notepaper and wrote as he talked on the phone. "Bulldozer . . . right. Demolition ball . . . okay. Two cranes . . . well, how much?"

When Augustus wasn't facing them, Grandpa and Cousin Dinky tried to sneak off the desk. But when he turned to them to hang up the phone, they froze into toy poses again.

"*Umm!*" said Augustus as he looked at Grandpa and Cousin Dinky. "There's something strange about these toys. I could swear they were over there . . . and now . . . they're over here." He reached out a hand to pick up the "toys."

Tom said, "Henry — save them!"

Quick as a flash, Henry knocked over a lamp. *Crash!!*

Augustus turned way from Grandpa and Cousin Dinky. "What the . . . ?"

"Grandpa! Dinky! Are you all right?" asked Lucy.

"Yes, thank heavens!" Grandpa said. "That was a close call. Now, let's get out of here."

"Let's find the airplane," suggested Cousin Dinky, "and see if it can be repaired."

Henry — still hidden — put Tom and Lucy on the floor. "Hide!" he said. "And, good luck!"

Augustus saw Henry's feet behind the chair. He reached down and grabbed the boy and pulled him out. "So," he said. "Now you're spying on me!" He dragged Henry to the door. "This time I'm going to *lock* you in your room."

As soon as the two big people were out of the room, Tom and Lucy rushed over to the desk. Grandpa and Cousin Dinky climbed down to meet them.

THE LITTLES found the toy airplane in the tall grass where it had crashed. It was quite badly damaged. Cousin Dinky thought it might take some time to do the repairs. They decided to find the cat and harness him to the plane. The cat could drag the plane to the garage. At least they would be safe there from any attack by night animals.

Just as they were ready to move the plane, Augustus came out of the house. He had looked out the window and seen the lawn mower still in the grass.

"That stupid Henry forgot to put a valuable piece of machinery back where it belongs," said Augustus to himself. He walked toward the mower. The Littles were close by in the tall grass.

"Get that cat going, Tom!" said Grandpa.

Tom ran to the cat's head and climbed the string to the harness. Then he stuck his face into the cat's ear and barked.

The cat ran toward the garage. The toy plane bumped along behind. Tom kept on barking. The cat scooted through the garage door and dived behind some boxes.

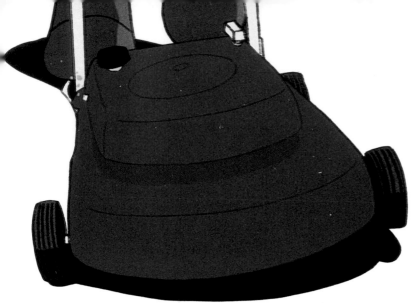

"We're safe," said Cousin Dinky. "Good work, Tom!"

"Hold it!" said Grandpa. He cocked his ear. "Hear that?"

The Littles listened. They could hear Augustus talking to himself. He was pushing the lawn mower to the garage.

"Oh, no!" said Lucy.

"He's bringing that thing in *here*!" Tom said.

Clunk!! There was a loud noise as Augustus angrily slammed the mower into a rock. "Blast it!" he yelled. "Can't see a thing — too dark."

The angry man pushed the mower into the garage, then walked out. He hadn't noticed — nor did the Littles see it — but there was a tiny rupture in the lawn mower's gas tank. The rock had done its damage. The gas began to trickle out of the hole and onto the garage floor.

"Let's get some light in here," said Cousin Dinky.

"How?" said Grandpa. "We don't dare use the garage lights."

"Well, I can't see to repair the plane in the dark," Cousin Dinky said.

Just then a bat swooped down from the rafters of the garage. For a moment it flew back and forth in front of the cat. The cat leaped after the bat, knocking a box off a shelf and onto the garage floor. Then the bat flew out the door with the cat after it.

"Look!" said Lucy. She pointed to a candle and some matches that had fallen out of the box.

The Littles rolled the candle to the plane and stood it up. Grandpa struck a match and lighted it. "Let's get to work, Dinky," he said.

But Cousin Dinky was on his hands and knees near the knocked-over trash bag. He was looking at scraps of paper. "Hey — there's

more of this stuff," he said. "Look — it's just like the writing I saw in Augustus's desk. He's writing the same letters over and over again."

"Fix the airplane, Dinky," said Grandpa. "We need a mechanic, not a detective."

"If we're going to be here a long time," said Lucy, "I'm going to need some food. I'm hungry."

"Me too," said Tom. "We haven't had anything to eat since yesterday."

"If we could just get into old Augustus's kitchen," said Lucy, "we might find something."

"You can," Grandpa said. He pointed to a hole in the garage wall. "That leads to a water pipe that leads to the kitchen. Follow the

pipe and you'll see a crack in the kitchen tile."

Tom and Lucy headed for the hole.

Grandpa and Cousin Dinky turned their attention to the airplane. Unknown to them, the gas tank on the lawn mower continued leaking slowly. A tiny stream of gas was making its way in the direction of the candle.

Tom and Lucy peeked into Augustus's kitchen through a crack in the tile counter.

Augustus was standing at the counter near the sink. He put some honey from a half-filled jar on a piece of bread. There was some leftover bread on the counter next to the honey jar.

As soon as the old man left the kitchen, Tom and Lucy climbed through the crack to the counter.

"I'd love to put some honey on that bread!" said Tom.

"The jar is too high," said Lucy.

"We need to do the old spoon trick," Tom said. He found a spoon nearby and dragged it to the jar. He pointed the bowl of the spoon toward the jar. The handle was away from it.

Then Tom stood on the handle. "Okay, Lucy," he said. "You know what to do."

Lucy climbed up onto a smaller jar and stood over the spoon. "Ready?" she asked.

"Ready!" Tom answered.

Lucy jumped onto the bowl of the spoon. The handle snapped upward. Tom shot into the air toward the jar. He landed on the lid. But the lid was loose and the tiny boy stumbled for a second and then toppled into the honey.

"Tom!" yelled Lucy. "Get out of there!"

"I can't," yelled Tom from inside the honey jar. He was standing on his toes, on the bottom of the jar. He was up to his chin in honey. Tom reached up, trying to grab the rim, but he couldn't.

Lucy heard footsteps approaching. "It's Augustus," she said. "Oh, Tom — what'll you do?" She ducked behind a cannister on the counter.

Augustus entered the room. Tom held his breath, closed his eyes, and lowered his head until he was completely under the honey.

The old man went to the counter, and poured himself a cup of coffee. On his way out, he tightened the lid on the honey jar. Then he left the room.

Tom came to the surface sputtering. He tried to wipe the honey from his face.

Lucy ran to the honey jar. "I'll get Grandpa and Cousin Dinky," she said. "We'll be right back."

"I'm not going anywhere," said Tom, making a sour face.

Lucy hurried to the crack in the tile.

In a few minutes the three Littles were standing beside the honey jar.

"It's hopeless," Grandpa said. "We can't possibly open the lid ourselves."

"That settles it," said Lucy. "We'll have to get help from Henry."

"Lucy!" scolded Grandpa. "There'll be no such talk. You know the rules about that."

"There's something I have to tell you," said Lucy, trying not to look Grandpa in the eyes. "Henry already knows about us."

"What?!" roared Grandpa.

"He discovered us," said Lucy.

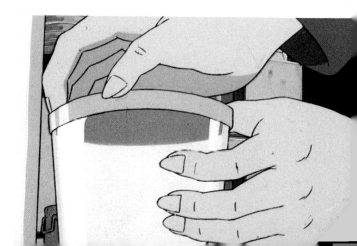

"We were talking too loud and forgetting where we were — and he saw us."

"I'm terribly ashamed of you kids," said Cousin Dinky. "He'll tell everyone and we'll have thousands of big people looking for tiny people."

"He *promised* not to," said Lucy. "And I believe him. Tom does too. Henry already helped us to find you when you were prisoners in the desk."

"Well, Tom is in a terrible fix, if you ask me," said Cousin Dinky. "We could sure use some help from *someone*." He looked at Grandpa.

"I suppose you're right," said Grandpa. "As long as Henry already knows, *and* promises not to tell any more big people — if he really is willing to help, we should probably use him in this situation."

"Maybe we can help him sometime," said Cousin Dinky. "It'll help him to keep the secret."

"Henry's locked in his room, remember?" said Cousin Dinky.

"Then we'll just have to get him out," said Grandpa. He started for the crack in the tile. "Come on, Dinky. We'll get that key from Augustus . . . somehow."

"Hurry!" Lucy said. "I'll go through the walls and meet you in Henry's room."

GRANDPA, Cousin Dinky, and Lucy entered Augustus's room through a wall grate. The old man was dressed in his night shirt. He was sitting in a chair, writing in a book.

"Drat!" said Grandpa. "He's still awake."

Augustus yawned loudly.

"That's a good sign," said Grandpa.

"Maybe he'll go to sleep soon," said Lucy.

"That book he's writing in," Cousin Dinky said. "It looks like some kind of diary."

"Never mind that," said Grandpa. "We need to get the key to Henry's room."

As soon as Augustus fell asleep, Grandpa and Cousin Dinky found the key to Henry's room on the end table. They carried it down the table leg to the floor.

"Now let's get up to Henry's room," said Grandpa.

"I'd still like to know what Augustus was writing in that book," Cousin Dinky said.

"Forget that book, will you?" said Grandpa. "Help me with this key. Tom is in big trouble."

At that moment Augustus moved an arm in his sleep, and knocked the book from his lap to the floor. It landed with a noise.

Grandpa looked up at Augustus to see if the noise had awakened him. He was still sleeping.

Cousin Dinky was lying on his back under the book. He looked up at it and read something. "Wow!" he said "It's a diary just like I thought, and it proves something I've been wondering about."

Grandpa said, "Dinky! Tom is drowning in a jar of honey and you're reading a book!"

Cousin Dinky ripped the page from the book. He rolled it up and stuck it under his arm. "This is evidence," he said. "I'm showing it to Henry."

"Grab the other end of this key," said Grandpa, "and let's get going. We've wasted enough time."

When the two men got to Henry's room, Lucy was already there waiting for them.

"This is Henry," she said, pointing up to the big boy. "He's our friend. He'll help us. Henry, this is Grandpa and Cousin Dinky."

Grandpa waved a hand at Henry. "I never thought I'd see the day when a Little talked to a Bigg," he said.

"It's okay," said Henry. "I promised Tom and Lucy I'd never tell anyone — not even my parents when they're found."

"I believe you, son," said Grandpa. "I've known you all your life and you've always been a good boy."

"We're wasting time talking," said Cousin Dinky. "Let's get to Tom."

Henry nodded. "I can carry all of you to the kitchen as soon as I get this door opened," he said. He took the key and opened the door.

"All aboard, Henry," said Grandpa.

Henry carefully picked up the

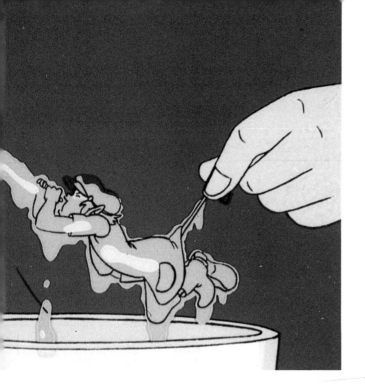

three Littles and carried them to the kitchen. He put them on the counter. They could see Tom at the bottom of the jar.

Henry unscrewed the top. He reached into the jar and pulled Tom out. He put him on the counter. Tom was covered from top to bottom with honey. It dripped from him slowly. His eyes were closed.

"Say something, Tom," said Grandpa.

"Are you all right?" asked Cousin Dinky.

Tom reached up slowly and wiped the honey from his face. He opened his eyes. "I've had enough honey to last my entire life," he said.

Lucy rushed to Tom and hugged him. "Oh, Tom!" she said. "I'm so happy." Now she was covered with honey too.

"I'd better wash you two off," said Henry. He picked up the two sticky children and held them under a running faucet.

Grandpa grabbed the rolled-up piece of paper from under Cousin Dinky's arm. "We can dry them off with this," he said.

"Not on your life!" said Cousin Dinky. He snatched the paper back from Grandpa. "This is important evidence that shows Augustus is trying to cheat Henry. It's a page from his diary."

"What?" said Henry. "Let me see that."

Cousin Dinky spread the paper on the counter. Henry looked it over. His eyes almost popped out of his head. "Holy cow!" he said. "It says my father *didn't* make Uncle Augustus my guardian."

Tom was reading the paper too. "And it says your father never gave Augustus permission to tear down *our* house!" he said.

"He *forged* my father's signature!" Henry went on.

"That crummy Augustus is even worse than I thought," Grandpa said.

Cousin Dinky was smiling. "I *told* you it was important," he said. "When Augustus was writing the same letters over and over again, he was practicing writing Mr. Bigg's name."

"So he could fool the authorities," said Tom.

"I should have listened to you, Dinky," said Grandpa. "You were right."

Lucy patted Cousin Dinky on the back. "You're practically a detective," she said. "I'm so proud of you, Cousin Dinky."

"*Now* we've got something to help us stop Augustus," said Grandpa.

"While we fly home," said Tom, "Henry can go to the police with this evidence."

Henry carried the Littles into the garage. No one noticed the tiny stream of gas from the leaking lawn mower. It had almost reached the low-burning candle.

Henry placed the Littles in the airplane's cockpit.

"Do you know where the police station is, Henry?" asked Grandpa.

"I think so," said Henry. "I'm pretty sure. I'll ask someone on the way. And I'll ride this old bike." He went over to the bicycle that was leaning against the garage wall and hopped on.

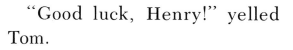

"Good luck, Henry!" yelled Tom.

Henry pedaled out of the garage and into the dark night.

"Okay, Dinky," said Grandpa. "Let's get this crate airborne."

"Roger!" said Cousin Dinky. He bent over the controls.

Just then Lucy saw the glittering stream of gasoline. It was surrounding the low candle. "Oh!" she said a second before it blew up.

Bang! ! !

Flames and smoke filled the garage.

"Get the plane out of here!" yelled Grandpa.

Cousin Dinky started the engine with a roar. The plane rolled toward the open garage door, picking up speed. It rose into the air through the smoke and flew out.

"We're safe!" yelled Lucy.

The plane zoomed upward.

Henry heard the explosion and rode back to the garage as fast as he could. He put out the fire with a garden hose. There was no trace of the Littles.

Just then he heard a faint buzzing above. He looked up and saw a tiny airplane off in the direction of his house.

"The Littles made it!" he cried. "But they'll need help. I've got to get to the police." He pedaled off.

Hours later — during the early dawn — Henry was still on the road. Only by this time he was pushing the bike; a tire had gone flat. He was talking to himself. "I'm lost. I must have made a wrong turn somewhere."

Henry heard a car coming. When it came into view, he held his hands up and shouted, "Help! Stop!"

The car came to a halt. Henry ran up to it as the door opened. "Please," he said. "Can you tell me how to get to the police station?"

An arm reached out and grabbed Henry. It was Augustus!

The old man was grinning. "I saw it all, boy," he said. "I stood in the window and saw you leave on the bike after setting the garage on fire. And now I've found you. You're going to be the sorriest boy that ever lived."

He tried to pull Henry into the car — but Henry managed to slip out of his uncle's grip.

Henry ran off down the road. "Run all you like!" Augustus yelled after him. "It will do you no good. In one half hour you'll have no place to run to. That's when I'll be at your house watching the bull-dozer tear it down!"

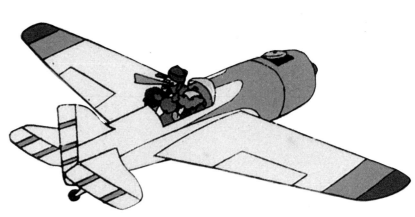

WITH Cousin Dinky at the controls of the airplane, the Littles flew in over the Biggs' roof. The first rays of the rising sun glinted off the plane's wings.

Lucy pointed down. "There's the bulldozer," she said.

Cousin Dinky landed the airplane near the house. Grandpa hopped out. "I'll find the folks," he said. "Dinky, you and the kids try to stop the bulldozer . . . somehow." He ran toward the house.

Cousin Dinky turned to Tom and Lucy. "Well, we know what the job is: We have to stop a *bulldozer*. Any ideas?"

"The only way we might be able to stop it," Tom said, "is to get inside where the motor is and pull out the right wires."

"Okay — good idea," said Cousin Dinky. "You kids get aboard the bulldozer and do what you can do. I'll attack it from the air. I may be able to bother the driver so he makes a mistake."

Tom and Lucy jumped out of the plane and ran off toward the bulldozer.

At the same time, Cousin Dinky took off and started diving at the monstrous machine.

Inside the bulldozer Tom and Lucy found a maze of multicolored cables, gears, wires, and whirring belts.

"Look at this motor," Tom said. "How do we stop it?"

"By pulling the right wires, you said," Lucy answered. "Which are the right ones, Tom?"

"How do I know?" said Tom.

"Well, we *have* to do *something!*" said Lucy. She pointed to a wire. "I have a feeling this is the one."

"Lucy! You can't go by feelings!" Tom said. "We have to be more *scientific* than that. Let's see. . . ."

In the meantime, Grandpa was in the Biggs' house. He found the Littles' alarm bell inside the wall.

"Mayday! Mayday!" yelled Grandpa. "Emergency! Will! Wilma! Come quickly!"

In a few moments Mr. and Mrs. Little came running down one of the wall passageways.

"What's wrong?" said Mr. Little.

"Where are the children?" asked Mrs. Little.

"They're okay," Grandpa said. "Hurry — we have to get out of this house — fast!"

Meanwhile, Cousin Dinky was still attacking the slowly moving bulldozer. As the tiny plane came in at an angle, the windshield of the bulldozer loomed up in front.

Crash! The plane bounced off the windshield. It flipped over backward three times and fell to the ground right in front of the giant machine.

The tiny pilot was thrown from the plane. He lay on the ground, unconscious, between the bulldozer and the house.

Grandpa, Mr. Little, and Mrs. Little came out just in time to see the crash.

Grandpa ran forward. "Dinky — get up!" he called. "Get out of there! You'll be killed!"

Cousin Dinky woke up. He felt the ground shaking.

The giant scooper was inches away. Dinky saw Grandpa and the Littles running toward him. He threw up his arms. "No — get back! Get back!" he cried.

At the very last second, the bull-dozer halted, its motor sputtering to a stop.

"What's this?" said Augustus. He saw Henry in the car. The boy was pointing at him.

Augustus walked boldly up to the police officers. He was smiling his creepiest smile. "Thank you, officers," he said. "I see you've captured the boy."

An officer leaped from the car and grabbed Augustus. He snapped some handcuffs on him.

"What are you doing?" screamed Augustus. "It's the *boy* you want! He set fire to my garage — stole my bicycle."

"You can stop lying, old man," said the policeman calmly. "We've seen evidence in your own handwriting that'll put you behind bars for five years."

Just then a car came up the driveway. It screeched to a stop. Augustus jumped out and ran to the bulldozer. "Get that thing going!" he commanded.

"The motor conked out," said the operator.

"Then fix it, you fool!" yelled Augustus.

But it was too late. In the next moment, a police car with siren going and lights flashing came tearing around the corner and up to the house.

Later, in the Littles' apartment, the family was listening at the grate to Henry's room.

"Hurry, Mrs. Evans," said Henry. "We have to get to the airport to meet my mom and dad."

Mrs. Evans entered the room. She hugged Henry. "I just knew your mother and father would be found," she said.

Henry looked around. "And our home is still here," he said. He pulled the rabbit's foot from his pocket. "Thanks to my lucky rabbit's foot." Then he looked over at the grate where the Littles were watching. "If it hadn't been in my suitcase, I wouldn't have had any help." He winked at the Littles.

Henry and Mrs. Evans walked out of the room.

"Now we can finally relax," said Grandpa. He fell into a chair.

"Tom and Lucy — I'm so proud of you," said Mr. Little. "If you hadn't stopped the bulldozer when you did, I hate to think of what would have happened to us . . . to the house . . . to everything."

"You know," said Grandpa, "for a moment I thought it was Dinky who had stopped the bulldozer."

"It surely looked that way," said Mrs. Little. "It stopped when he held his hands up."

"I thought it was a miracle," said Cousin Dinky.

"*Now,* Tom," said Lucy. "You

have to tell us how you figured out which wire to pull."

"Aw, heck!" Tom said. "It wasn't much. Maybe Cousin Dinky was right; maybe it was a miracle."

"No, no!" said Lucy. "It was *scientific*. You said so yourself. I saw you going from one wire to another and mumbling something to yourself. What was it?"

Everyone was looking at Tom.

"Well," he said. Then he grinned. "I really didn't know *what* to do."

"You're being modest, Tom," said Grandpa. "Tell us how you figured it out."

"I said . . ." Tom began pointing with his finger. "I said: 'Eeny, meeny, miney, moe!'"

All the Littles laughed.

Grandpa laughed so long and hard he leaned back in his chair, the leg broke, and he fell on the floor.

He was still laughing when everybody ran to help him up.